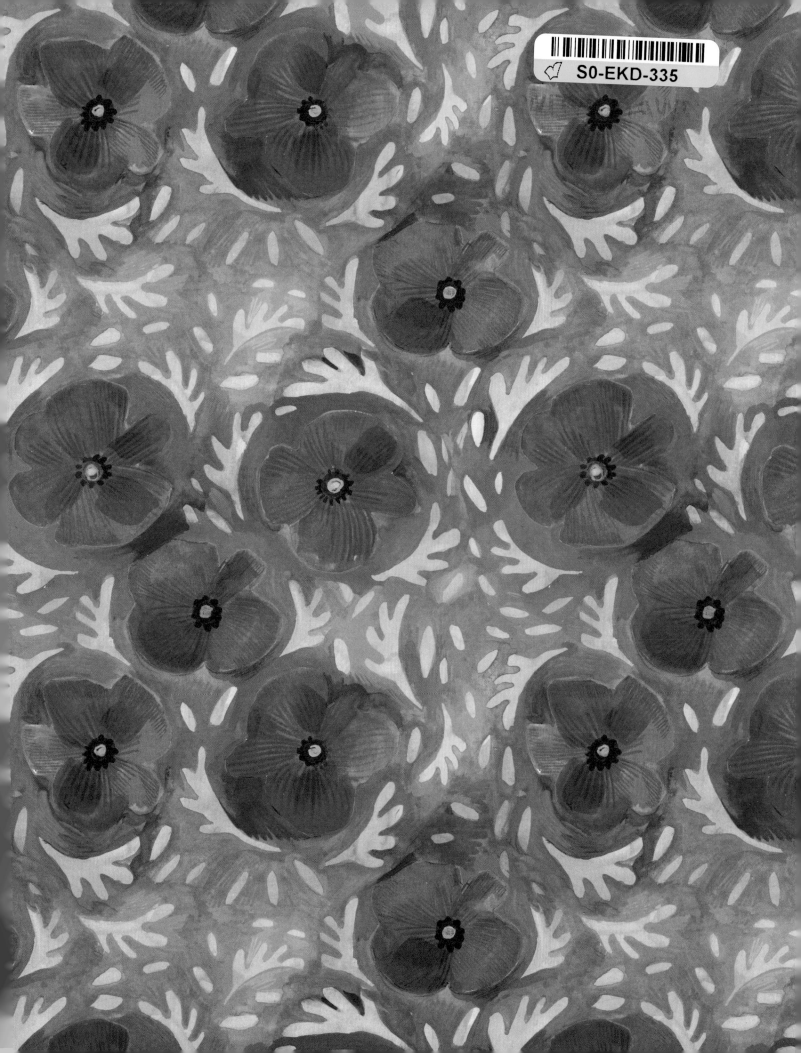

SERGEANT BILLY

The True Story of
THE GOAT
Who Went to War

Mireille Messier   Illustrated by Kass Reich

tundra

To Susan C., who loves goats.
And to all the service animals
and those who love them.
—MM

To my dad, the history buff of the family: thanks for keeping
this decorated war goat historically accurate and for helping me
with anything else I've needed over the years. —KR

Tundra Books, an imprint of Penguin Random House Canada
Young Readers, a Penguin Random House Company

Library and Archives Canada Cataloguing in Publication

Messier, Mireille, 1971–, author
    Sergeant Billy : the true story of the goat who went to war
/ Mireille Messier ; illustrated by Kass Reich.
Issued in print and electronic formats.
ISBN 978-0-7352-6442-7 (hardcover).
ISBN 978-0-7352-6443-4 (EPUB)
    1. Sergeant Billy (Goat)—Juvenile literature. 2. World War,
1914–1918—Juvenile literature. 3. Animals—War use—
Canada—History—20th century—Juvenile literature. I. Reich,
Kass, illustrator
II. Title.
D639.A65M48 2019   j940.4'12710929   C2018-906280-0
                                        C2018-906281-9

Published simultaneously in the United States of America
by Tundra Books of Northern New York, an imprint of
Penguin Random House Canada Young Readers,
a Penguin Random House Company

Library of Congress Control Number: 2018962669

Edited by Samantha Swenson
Designed by Leah Springate
The artwork in this book was hand-painted in gouache with
details added digitally.
The text was set in Century Schoolbook.

Printed and bound in China

www.penguinrandomhouse.ca

1 2 3 4 5   23 22 21 20 19

Photo credits:
Front flap and page 39: CWM 1993003-388, George Metcalf
Archival Collection, Canadian War Museum.
Page 40 (top): CWM 20020045-1450, George Metcalf Archival
Collection, Canadian War Museum; (upper middle): photograph
courtesy Broadview Museum Saskatchewan; (lower middle,
bottom left and right): photographs courtesy Ernest Swanston
and family. Many thanks to all!

Sources:
Broadview Museum: www.broadviewmuseum.weebly.com/ser-
geant-bill
The Canadian Veterinary Journal: www.ncbi.nlm.nih.gov/pmc/
articles/PMC1686686
Veterans Affairs Canada: www.veterans.gc.ca/eng/remem-
brance/information-for/students/tales-of-animals-in-war/2013/
goat
Scientific American (blog): www.blogs.scientificamerican.com/
tetrapod-zoology/military-goats
Storey: https://www.storey.com/article/sue-weaver-animals-who-
served-for-our

A train full of soldiers made a stop in a small prairie town.

In that town, there was a girl named Daisy with a goat named Billy.

"Mind if we borrow your goat?" one of the soldiers asked Daisy.

Daisy almost said no. She was very fond of her goat. But the soldiers were going to war and they thought Billy would bring them luck. So Daisy said yes — as long as they brought Billy back after the war. The soldiers promised they would.

And that's how Billy's extraordinary story began.

During the long ride to training camp, Billy climbed on the seats, the luggage and the soldiers' laps, to the delight of most of the men.

By the time they reached their destination, the soldiers of the Fifth Battalion had become very fond of Billy.

"He's one of us now! An army goat. Let's call him *Private* Billy!"

And that's how Billy joined the army.

When the soldiers trained, Private Billy did too.
He marched, crawled and ran with the best of
them. When a soldier lagged behind, Private Billy
knew how to get him back with the pack.

Soon it was time to ship out to England and join the fight. The colonel ordered Billy to stay. But the soldiers of the Fighting Fifth had grown so attached to their goat that they didn't want to leave him behind. So they snuck him on board.

And that's how Private Billy crossed the ocean.

As the war raged on and enemy troops advanced,
the Fifth Battalion was sent from England to
France to fight on the front lines.

Mascots were strictly forbidden at the front. And since the soldiers had already snuck Billy over to England without permission, the colonel was watching them extra closely.

But the Fighting Fifth was determined. "We can easily find another colonel, but we'll never find another Billy!"

So they bought a huge wooden crate of oranges, ate and sold all the fruit, and then used the empty crate to smuggle Private Billy into France.

And that's how Private Billy went to the front lines.

Unlike many of the soldiers, Private Billy
took well to life in the trenches.

He didn't mind the mud.

Or the cold.

Or the noise.

Or the foul food.

Or even the rats.

Private Billy was by the soldiers' sides in victory and defeat. He was the first to befriend the nervous new recruits and to comfort those who missed their fallen friends.

Instead of writing about their own hard times, the soldiers often wrote about Private Billy in letters to their loved ones back home.

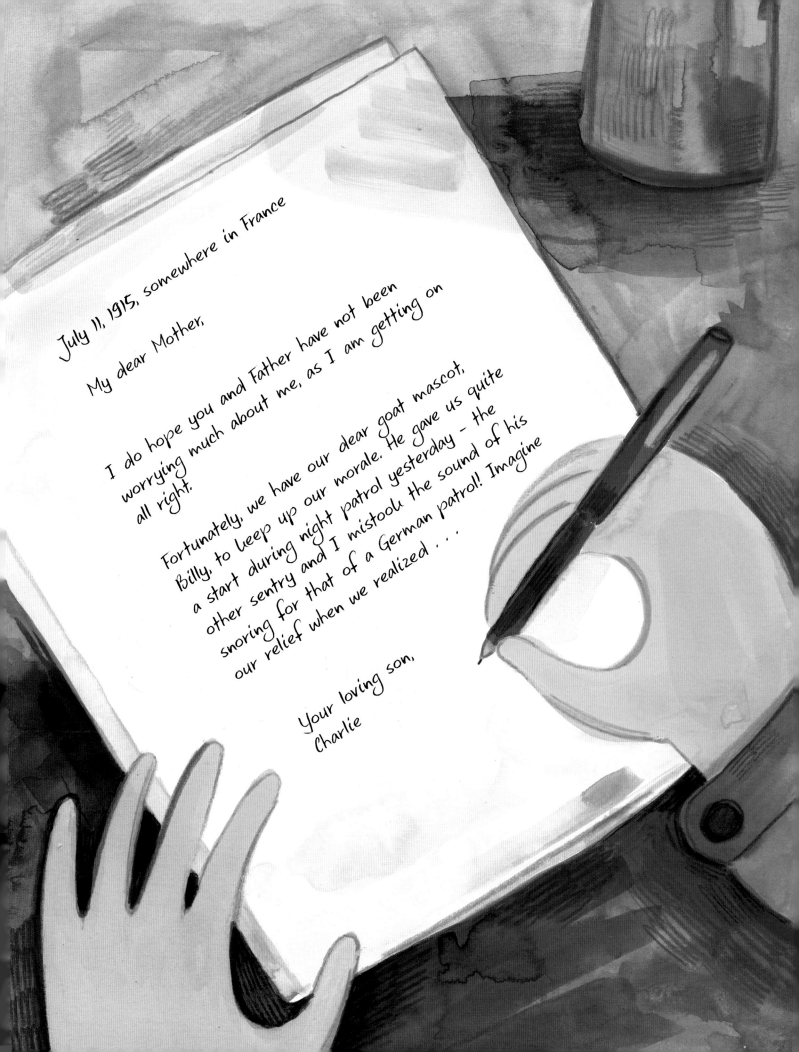

July 11, 1915, somewhere in France

My dear Mother,

I do hope you and Father have not been worrying much about me, as I am getting on all right.

Fortunately, we have our dear goat mascot, Billy, to keep up our morale. He gave us quite a start during night patrol yesterday — the other sentry and I mistook the sound of his snoring for that of a German patrol! Imagine our relief when we realized . . .

Your loving son,
Charlie

Still, there were some, including the colonel, who did not think a goat belonged in the trenches.

"We have no food or space to spare!" he said.

But Private Billy wasn't picky. If the food rations were low, he ate whatever he could find.

Once, he was even caught nibbling on some very
important secret documents.

"This is treason!" the colonel declared.

So he placed the goat under arrest.

And that's how Private Billy went to jail for
being a spy.

Without Billy to rally around, the soldiers were
unhappy. They fought with each other and were
bored and grumpy. The colonel was perplexed. All this
because they missed their goat?

So Private Billy was forgiven and returned to the
Fifth Battalion.

Private Billy became instrumental in battle —
even the colonel had to agree.

And that's how Private Billy was promoted
to sergeant.

At Ypres, Sergeant Billy captured an enemy guardsman.

At Hill 63, Sergeant Billy got trench foot.

At Hill 70, Sergeant Billy was shell-shocked.

At Festubert, Sergeant Billy boldly saved some soldiers' lives by head-butting them into a trench seconds before a shell exploded right where they had been standing.

No matter how hard things got, the soldiers always looked after Billy . . . and Billy always looked out for his soldiers.

"For exceptional bravery in the face of danger, the Mons Star is awarded to Sergeant Billy of the Fifth Battalion!"

And that's how Sergeant Billy became a decorated war hero.

Months, seasons and years passed. Not everyone survived. But Billy was still with the Fighting Fifth when the roar of the cannons finally stopped.

"The war is over!"

"Thank our lucky goat!"

"Three cheers for Sergeant Billy!"

The voyage back was long, but the soldiers of
the Fighting Fifth had a promise to keep. So,
with feverish hearts, they crossed the hundreds
of miles of smoldering land and the hundreds of
miles of stormy sea.

And that's how Billy came home.